PUFFIN BOOKS

The Witch's Dog at the
School of Spells

Frank Rodgers has written and illustrated a wide range of books for children: picture books, story books, how-to-draw books and a novel for teenagers. His work for Puffin includes the highly popular *Intergalactic Kitchen* series and the picture books *The Bunk-Bed Bus* and *The Pirate and the Pig*. He was an art teacher for a number of years before becoming an author and illustrator. He lives in Glasgow with his wife and two children.

D0201699

Some other books by Frank Rodgers

THE WITCH'S DOG

THE INTERGALACTIC KITCHEN SINKS

Picture books

THE BUNK-BED BUS
THE SHIP-SHAPE SHOP
THE PIRATE AND THE PIG

Frank Rodgers

The Witch's Dog
at the School
of Spells

PUFFIN BOOKS

PUFFIN BOOKS

Published by the Penguin Group
Penguin Books Ltd, 27 Wrights Lane, London W8 5TZ, England
Penguin Putnam Inc., 375 Hudson Street, New York, New York 10014, USA
Penguin Books Australia Ltd, Ringwood, Victoria, Australia
Penguin Books Canada Ltd, 10 Alcorn Avenue, Toronto, Ontario, Canada M4V 3B2
Penguin Books (NZ) Ltd, 182–190 Wairau Road, Auckland 10, New Zealand

Penguin Books Ltd, Registered Offices: Harmondsworth, Middlesex, England

First published 1998
1 3 5 7 9 10 8 6 4 2

Typeset in Times New Roman Infants

Printed in Hong Kong by Midas Printing Limited

British Library Cataloguing in Publication Data
A CIP catalogue record for this book is available from the British Library

ISBN 0–140–38467–7

W ilf was a witch's dog.
He enjoyed helping Weenie
the witch with her magic spells . . .

. . . and she enjoyed using her spells to help others.

"Would you teach me to make
spells?" asked Wilf.
"Of course!" said Weenie.

"We'll start with this flying spell."

She told Wilf what he must do.

He put his fingers in his ears . . .

puffed
out his
cheeks . . .

crossed
his eyes . . .

and thought of the spell.

Slowly he rose in the air.

He turned upside down . . .

and shot backwards . . .

knocking over his friends
who had just arrived.

"What do you think you're doing,
Wilf?" gasped Harry.
"A flying spell," said Wilf.

"I think you need to go back to
school," laughed Streaky,
"and learn *how* to spell!"

"School!" gasped
Weenie. "That
reminds me! I got
a letter from
the School of
Spells this
morning."

"Look at this, Wilf," she said.

Dear Weenie,
Your spells are now the best in town. Please come and be a teacher at the School of Spells.

"That's wonderful!"
said Wilf.
"Can I come
with you,
Weenie?"

"Of course you can!" said Weenie.
"I'm sure you'll learn quickly."

"He'd better," grinned Bertie.
"I don't want to be knocked over
again."

At the School of Spells, Wilf was
delighted to be in Weenie's class.

But Sly Cat and Tricky Toad were
also in her class. They were jealous
of Wilf because he had won the
"Witch's Pet of the Year"
competition.

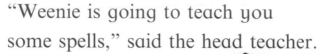

"Weenie is going to teach you
some spells," said the head teacher.

"And at the end of the week I want
you all to show me how you've used
them."

14

Sly looked at Tricky.
"Let's make a mess of Wilf's
spells," he whispered.

"Good idea," said Tricky.

"Now, class," said
Weenie, "the first
lesson is a
disappearing spell."

She wrote the spell on the
blackboard and everyone copied
it into their jotters.

16

Sly winked at Tricky and knocked
his pencils on to the floor. They
scattered everywhere.

"Let me help you pick these
up," said Wilf.

As they were busy picking up the pencils, Tricky hopped over and changed the spell in Wilf's book.

Then everyone tried the spell.

At first they weren't very
good . . .

but they soon got better.

Wilf couldn't
do it at all!
He tried and
tried but instead
of disappearing . . .

he turned yellow and blue
with purple spots!

Sly and Tricky
snorted with
laughter.

"Don't worry, Wilf," said Weenie
with a smile as she brought him
back to normal. "You'll soon get
the hang of it."

But next day was just as bad.
Everybody else managed to do the
lifting spell except Wilf. Sly and
Tricky had changed the spell in his
book again.

Instead of lifting his
books into the air
Wilf grew a long tail . . .

and knocked off the
head teacher's wig.

She was not amused,
but Sly and Tricky
thought it was
very funny.

Next day was even worse. When they tried the shrinking spell, all the pets became tiny except Wilf. He became an enormous dinosaur . . .

and nearly sat on the head
teacher!

"Weenie!" she
shouted. "Could
you kindly control
your pet!"

Weenie and Wilf were worried. The rest of the class were now using their spells and had helped lots of people.

Wilf had tried and tried . . .

but he hadn't even managed
to do one spell.

"I'll never be a proper witch's dog if I don't get my spells to work," said Wilf sadly that night.

"You just need to practise," said Weenie. "Let me see your jotter."

"These spells are wrong, Wilf," she gasped. "Someone has changed them!"

"I think I
know who,"
said Wilf.

"Never mind,"
said Weenie.
"I'll correct
them for you."

They practised all evening . . .

. . . and next day Wilf was wonderful.
He disappeared with a *POP* . . .

shrank to the
size of a flea . . .

and lifted his books, desk and chair into the air!

Everyone cheered . . . except Sly and Tricky.

"Marvellous!" said Weenie. "There is only the flying spell to learn and you can start helping people, Wilf." Wilf was very happy.

Sly and Tricky
were furious but
Tricky thought
of a plan.
He whispered
it to Sly.

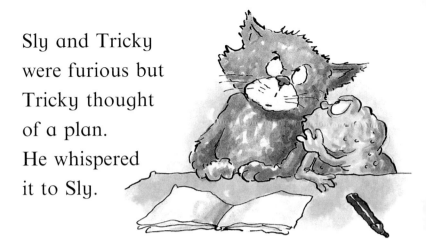

Sly grinned. "That sounds good,"
he said.

And giggling
together, they
sneaked off.

Weenie taught everyone the flying
spell. Toads, rats and cats flapped
round the playground.

Wilf was now getting the hang of it
too. Slowly he rose into the air.

But Sly and Tricky had come back
and they had a special book of
magic spells with them.

As Wilf rose higher, Sly said,
"Now!"

He and Tricky
read out a super-
strong flying
spell . . .

and aimed it straight at Wilf.

CRAAACKLE!

Blue lightning sparkled around
Wilf.

He hovered in mid-air for a
moment then . . .

WHOOOSH

He shot into the sky and in
a few seconds he was out of
sight.

38

Sly and Tricky rolled on the
ground, helpless with laughter.

"That's the last we'll see
of Wilf!" they jeered.

Just then, Wilf's friends
arrived.

"What have you two done with
Wilf?" demanded Bertie.

"E-er . . ." stammered Sly.
"Speak up!" said Harry.

40

Sly and Tricky confessed and Wilf's
friends ran to tell Weenie.

"A super-strong flying spell?" she
gasped. "That will send him a long
way!" She rushed off to get her
telescope.

Wilf was zooming through the
sky faster than a bird . . .

and even faster than a plane.

But at last the spell began
to wear off . . .

and down he came . . .

right into the middle
of a zoo!

"Who are you?"
asked the
zookeeper.

"I'm Wilf, the
witch's dog,"
said Wilf.

"Can you do magic?" asked
the keeper.

"Yes," said Wilf.
"Do you need any
help?"

"I certainly do," said the keeper.
"I've got two problems. The first
one is this bad-tempered rhino."

The rhino
shook its
head angrily.

"It's got a thorn in its ear," said the keeper. "And it won't let me take it out."

Wilf tried a spell.

FLASH!

He shrank
to the size
of a beetle . . .

climbed up on to the rhino's
back . . .

and went into
its ear.

It was like a deep, dark
cave.

Bravely, Wilf went
all the way to
the bottom . . .

and found the thorn.

He tugged
with all his
strength . . .

and pulled
it out!

"Brilliant!" said the keeper when
Wilf returned. "The rhino is happy
now."

"I'm glad," said Wilf. "Now,
what's the second problem?"

"My elephant," said the keeper. "It went into the pond for a paddle and can't get out. The sides are too slippery."

Wilf tried a lifting spell.
The elephant was very heavy
and at first it didn't move.

But then, very slowly, it
lifted out of the pond . . .

and landed gently beside
the keeper.

"Wilf, you're a
genius!" he cried.
"Thank you so
much for all
your help!"

At that moment,
Weenie saw Wilf
through her
telescope.

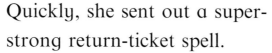

Quickly, she sent out a super-
strong return-ticket spell.

It flew as fast as light . . .

and hit
Wilf and the
zookeeper.

They both shot into the air . . .

. . . zoomed through the sky and
landed right beside Weenie
in the playground.

"Hooray!" shouted Bertie, Harry
and Streaky. "You're back safe
and sound!"

Sly and Tricky were fuming.
Not only had Wilf succeeded . . .

but when the head teacher found out
what they had done, she sent them
home in disgrace.

The zookeeper then told her how Wilf had helped him.

"Wilf!" she cried. "You are a wonderful witch's dog!

"And you, Weenie,
are a wonderful
witch!"
"Thank you," said
Weenie and Wilf.

Then Weenie sent the zookeeper
home and everybody cheered.

"Weenie is our favourite teacher!"
they cried. "And Wilf, the witch's
dog, is top of the class!"